I Like School

by Michaela Muntean
Illustrated by Tom Herbert

Featuring Jim Henson's Sesame Street Muppets

A SESAME STREET/GOLDEN PRESS BOOK
Published by Western Publishing Company, Inc.
in conjunction with Children's Television Workshop.

flag

STOP

bus

slide

playground

lunch box

window

calendar

bulletin board

poster

record player

desk

ABCDEFGHIJKLM

I like to write my name.

chalkboard

ERNIE
ERNIE
ERNIE
ERNIE

NOPQRSTUVWXYZ

alphabet

clock

BERT
BERT
BERT
BERT

chalk

eraser

book cart

bookshelf

librarian

library
card

book stamp

books

CHECK BOOKS
OUT HERE

RETURN BOOKS
HERE

raisins

plates

carrots

nuts

triangle

music book

piano

cymbals

storybook

jump rope

swing

seesaw

ball

seat

driver

steering wheel

HISTORY OF TRASH